FELIX
The Small Boy With The
Big Imagination

Copyright 2017
Lorna McCann

Illustrated by Holly Bushnell

© Lorna McCann 2017

First Published 2017

ISBN-13:978-1981279944

TEAMAUTHOR UK
Self-Publishing with you

This book belongs to

....

Dedication

For my wonderful, imaginative and curious boys
Lucas and Finn
xx

"Mummy, I want to be an explorer."
"Mummy, I want to be a deep sea diver."
"Mummy, I want to be a rock star."

Felix was a small boy with a BIG imagination and he loved dressing up.

Everyday Felix pretended to be someone different.

"Mummy, when I grow up I'm going to be a Morris dancer," he said, jiggling about with bells on his legs and clanking sticks together.

"Woo hoo!" he shouted.

Felix was a very observant little boy and everywhere he went, he watched other people very carefully, paying particular attention to the clothes they wore and the jobs they were doing.

"Today Mummy, I'm going to be a doctor," he said, pulling on his white overcoat and adjusting his shirt and tie.

"Do you need fixing, Mummy?"

But it was too late, Felix was already busy setting up his doctor's surgery.

"When I call your name, you can come into my room and I will make you better," he said.

Felix would lose himself in his imaginary games pretending to be a doctor or a vet, a pilot, a fireman or an astronaut.

And, when he got bored, he would make his way upstairs to his ENORMOUS dressing up box.

"Now Mummy, I'm a policeman," he shouted.

"Nee nah, nee nah!"

Felix was a small boy with a BIG imagination and he loved dressing up.

He didn't mind where he went or who saw him when he was dressed up.

He liked to be different and dressing up made him feel happy.

"Mummy, today I'm going to be a rock climber," he said, pulling on his rucksack and tying a rope around his waist.

"Do I make a good rock climber?"

"Yes, of course," said Mummy.

"You look just like the real thing."

But, by now Felix wasn't paying any attention. He was already climbing onto the sofa pretending it was the biggest mountain in the world.

"I can't quite reach the top," he shouted, tossing a rope over the back and pulling himself up.

Felix was a small boy with a BIG imagination and he loved dressing up.

"Mum!" he shouted.

"Will you help me dress up as a builder?"

Felix threw off his rucksack and dumped it in the middle of the floor and before Mum could say anything, he was off, clambering back upstairs to his ENORMOUS dressing up box.

"You know Felix," said Mummy, as she rummaged around trying to find his builder's hat and belt.

"Sometimes it's nice when you're just Felix. You're always pretending to be someone else."

"I know Mummy, but not today, I'm busy being a builder," he said hammering away.

"What would you like me to build for you?"

Felix was a small boy with a BIG imagination and he loved dressing up.

Felix and Mummy's tower

But, sometimes, dressing up was hard work.

"I'm tired," said Felix rubbing his eyes after his busy day
of being a Morris dancer, a doctor, a policeman, a rock
climber and a builder.

"Let's go and get ready for bed," said Mummy.

As Felix got undressed and into
his pyjamas, he said, "Mummy,
what can I be when I grow up?"

"You can be whatever you like,"
said Mummy.

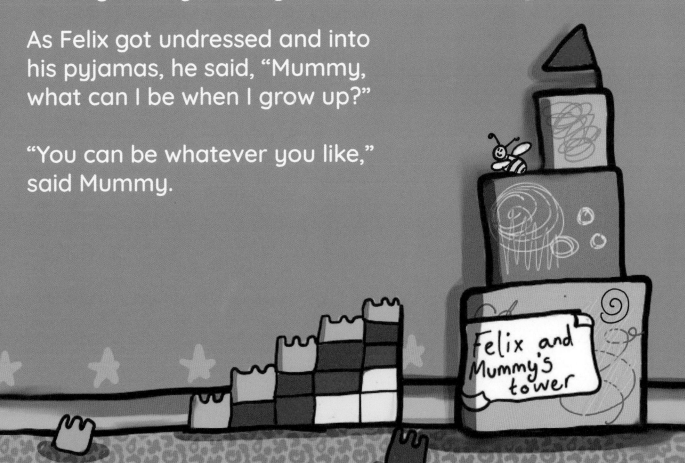

Felix and
Mummy's
tower

My Book of Adventures

Bedtime Stories for Boys

PHOTO ALBUM

I Love You ♥

Wendy and the Biscuit Tree

★ Astronaut Lamby ★

"Hmmm," thought Felix for a moment.

"I know Mummy, I'm going to be a soldier."

"No, wait!" he shouted.
"I've changed my mind, I'm going to be a BMX biker."

Felix was a small boy with a BIG imagination and he loved dressing up.

He hopped into bed and snuggled right under his covers. "Can you tuck me in please, Mummy?" he said quietly. "Of course I can," she said, leaning over and giving him a big kiss on the cheek.

"I'm sleepy, Mummy. It's hard work being a grown up," whispered Felix.

And with that, he gave a big yawn and fell fast asleep dreaming of the adventures he'd have tomorrow.

About the Author

Lorna McCann is a children's author based in Shropshire. She writes imaginative, engaging and fun tales for children aged 3 to 7 to enjoy anywhere at any time. Her stories and characters are brought to life with beautifully drawn and brightly coloured illustrations and Lorna hopes her books will encourage children to enjoy reading, writing and drawing for many years to come.

Lorna has always been a writer and started her professional career as a newspaper reporter in Shropshire. She then went on to write for various regional newspaper titles across the UK before moving into the PR industry writing content for a range of media and specialist publications. As well as being an author, Lorna now runs her own PR company and is part of the marketing team for TeamAuthorUK helping to provide PR services to other authors.

Lorna was inspired to start writing stories for children by her two sons, Lucas and Finn. Both her boys have always loved books and Lorna's made up tales. This is Lorna's second book to date. Her first 'Wendy and the Biscuit Tree' was published in 2016.

To follow Lorna and to find out more about her books and school author visits take a look at:

Lorna's website: https://lornamccann.wordpress.com
Facebook.com/lornamccannauthor
Send her an email: lorna.mccann@teamauthoruk.co.uk

About the Illustrator

Holly Bushnell is an artist and illustrator. She specialises in bespoke murals for schools, Nurseries, private commissions and bookshops. Holly is one of the illustrators for TeamAuthorUK and her pictures bring children's books alive.

Find out more about Holly at:
www.hollybushnelldesigns.co.uk

www.facebook.com/
hollybushnelldesigns

Acknowledgements

Huge thanks to the wonderful TeamAuthorUK especially editor Sue Miller for her support, kindness and constant encouragement. Thanks to Holly Bushnell for her time, creativity and beautiful illustrations.

Special thanks to my wonderful husband Matt for his never ending belief and finally lots of love to my two amazing boys Lucas and Finn. Thank you for your endless energy and inspiration!

Printed in Great Britain
by Amazon